Dark & Dangerous

By

Aron James McPhail

Prologue

Unfortunately, when you are next in line for the Throne, people expect you to follow certain traditions, one of them would be to marry someone of high social standing that is suited to be a husband of a Queen, I have watched so many people think their husband is suited for the family to behead them. Knowing the family are watching every move you make could have repercussions on me when I become queen, for me to escape becoming queen means that I would have to vacate any royal titles that was given to me. I know moving away from the family tradition means that they would not have to keep paying for any security that I may have, lucky for me when father passed away, I received some inheritance. The family did not like the idea that I wanted to be a strong independent woman with a voice, once the royal responsibilities had been given to other family members only then I was free from what ever came next within the family. Moving away from London to Seattle was not the smartest idea that I had produced, I ended up living with a nice gentleman. When the gentleman spoke, his voice was husky and sometimes harsh with me...

On arriving at the airport, I notice that I was sitting in economy class it had me disheartened that this is how the family has treated me after years of service to the country... Thankfully due to a friend putting me in contact with this gentleman, they were not helpful when asking about this gentleman... All they said was "he would be expecting me!"

While living with the gentleman I became his housekeeper. Even with the money that my father had left for me I was unable to have that in till I turned 20-years-old, so my only option was to clean for him the man made sure that whatever I needed was always there I never needed to ask for any cleaning products, the gentleman was never around. I would wonder exactly what he was up to. Sometimes the gentleman would come home with other women that would ask "who is she?" The gentleman would never answer back on who I was, it was only when we finely got a moment the gentleman asked, "what is your name?"

"My name sir is Emily Winters I come from London England sir."

While Luca was growing up, he never understood why he couldn't see his real family... The foster family he happened to be with at the time would put out their cigarettes on him, using him as a human ashtray Luca thought this was somewhat normal, he was only around six to seven years old when this would happen it was when he went to another family that he realised this was child abuse...

On occasion at night Luca would remove his top to look at the scarring, and when he closed his eyes, it would take him right back to that point in time...

"London you say? Cannot say I have ever heard of it, well, Emily my name is Luca Lavigne." Since being here, we had never spoken until now. Luca walked up right like he owned the world and every step he took had a meaning behind it, only what was the meaning? He had hazel brown eyes with blood orange hair and when he spoke to you there was a deep tone that pulled you in, I had been told story's that worried me, Luca has had many housekeepers before me. I was wanting to know more about him, but the only thing was he was never around until night-time and by then I was asleep. Knowing that Luca could be asleep in the room next to mine was nerve wracking.

I wondered how many people have been in this same bed that I am now in. I might never know that answer but what I am sure about is that I will not be the last, the night felt like it was never ending, as the sun came up, I fell to sleep knowing I would see him again.

When I woke there was a nice cup of tea on the side table with a note on it, asking me to drink it. How did he know what I liked in the mornings? There was something about waking up and seeing the tea, had he seen me make one or took a guess? Once more as I went to the kitchen, he cooked me American pancakes, he welcomed me as I was his wife Obviously, I was not going to look a gift horse in the mouth and turn away such a lovely gesture... but the intent look was like I want to know more about you, Lucas' house overlooks the streets off Seattle. "Have you ever been in love before Emily?" I replied, "do you mind, that is personal and has nothing to do with you, "sorry only asking a question!" He replied.

everything was coordinated within the house, "Luca? Hope you do not mind me asking but why do you keep people at a distance?" "For many reasons, one is that to understand me you would need to be a psychiatrist. Two, is that when people see the real me, they do not like what they see Emily, and to end this my wardrobe has many skeletons."

As she stands up from the breakfast bar revealing nothing but her black silk nightwear that hugged all the curves of her body, the inner carnal desires that every man has with in them wanted to ignite. She looks round with her light blue eyes meeting mine, only what caught my attention was how she bit down on her bottom lip, her mousy brown hair moved effortlessly as the wind blew through from the open balcony door. The attention was soon broken when her cell phone rang. Her voice was calming but soft when she spoke, she was unaware that I was listening, but I could not spend the day with her as much as it would have pleased me. There was a number of people I needed to see that owed me money and I couldn't let it go on any longer as it made me look weak and in my world Luca Lavigne is not fucking weak, things were going to get dark and dangerous today and people ARE going to get hurt and I couldn't drag her into this without her fully knowing what consequences came after.

The door shut as he headed out leaving me alone with nothing but my thoughts, I could not wait for him to come home so that I could see him. Something inside told me to dive right in and fuck the consequences, that might await me if I was to be involved with Luca. Then it dawned on me that I was nothing but his house keeper what was I thinking by surmising that he even wanted me, I was more than likely just another house keeper that won't be here for long. Luca burst in the door covered in blood, sending emotions running sky high, as I went over he stopped me and said "don't worry this is not my blood," as he said that I breathed a sigh of relief trying not to cry about the mess he was in. As he removed the top showing his abdomen, I hoped that he would not notice my blushing cheeks, lucky he walked away before I turned back round.

The sexual tension between us had to be subdued somehow, because if this keeps up, I might explode. "Emily? Would you like to come to dinner with me tonight?" When he asked, I was like "oh fuck yes," the moment had come that I was craving. I headed to the spare room that he had made into a dressing room for me I could not resist the silky white dress, that would have his eyes popping from his head. He took me to a little restaurant just outside off Seattle. "Look Emily? I have been waiting to ask you how you would feel about me kissing you?" as we were about to kiss, we were interrupted by his driver Paul, the night abruptly ended as he was called away. Luca needed to see someone in Portland he would not say what it was about, I guess he would tell me when he is home. Luca was going to be gone for about three days with what Paul was on about in the car, they would not go into detail as Luca keeps what he does away from me.

Those three days could not have gone any slower, when Luca walked through the door, he was acting very strange he then called me over. He ran his hands over his face before laying a long and passionate kiss on my lips, my heart began to race and I pressed myself into Lucas body, he softly pushed me back and explained that we did not have time, this was frustrating and left and me wanting "it" more. What we did not know was that the old housekeeper was keeping watch on what Luca was doing. I was told that when the old housekeeper was here, she had formed an obsession with Luca, her name was Zofia. What Luca was not informed of is that Zofia had mental health issues that were out his control.

When Zofia came to be in my company, she was only young and unknown to me, so when her obsession had taken over, I decided that her time working here was over. For years after she moved around Seattle telling anyone that would take any interest that I used her for sex, in the end Zofia had to be sectioned to get her the correct help that she needed. I was not told that she was out walking the streets again a feeling inside told me she would head here to see me, I knew then that Zofia had fallen in love with me but that is not what I wanted at the time.

When she was in the hospital, all that I could think of was that I had been leading her on and given her the wrong idea about us. What was she here to do? I had to stop that way of thinking. As Emily came walking with me, we were then confronted with Zofia she looked high on something, we were not going to upset her anymore then she was I moved Emily to the side as Zofia pulled a gun out. "Paul take Emily back to Escala?" "Are you crazy Fuck that shit!"

"Emily for once do as you are asked and not as you like!"

"Paul if she won't go with you carry her back to Escala!"

With Zofia holding Luca at gun point and Paul dragging me away, I was horrified of what could happen as we approached the car. We heard a gun shoot that echoed for miles. Paul ran back and Luca was crouched down, and the gun was smoking after the shot, but there was no Zofia. Paul looked around the immediate area to see if she was hiding but she was nowhere to be seen. We made it home safely but that wasn't to say the ordeal was over, how could we be sure she wasn't here with us right now? Paul made sure the house was secure before Luca would allow me back in the house, what we noticed was that someone had tampered with the CCTV monitors. It looked as if they had done it while we were out walking, we could not even reboot the system, once we were home it frustrated Paul and Luca.

Chapter 1

Later that night once the CCTV had rebooted. Luca entered the room his face was telling a story, but would he say what was vexing him? He walks on over rubbing his hands over his stubble, breathing heavily like he had been fighting with someone, he makes it known to me that my time here was up, "Luca has something happened that I don't know about?" Lucas eyes widened his face filled with anger I could not think of what had made him this angry, then before I could do anything Luca slapped me, "you are nothing but a lying BITCH that's what you are Emily!" The slap that Luca gave me could be felt from anywhere in the house he had not explained what I had done, "why didn't you tell me who you were when I so kindly took you in? You know I like you, but you have lied on one-to-many times Emily."

Luca called me a BITCH that came across strong or was it the slap he gave me, I could not decide on weather to cry or to ask Luca to explain himself for putting his hands on me. When Luca finely came to talk with me "Emily I'm sorry, I was high on snow." Luca slapped me so hard it gave me whiplash and left the side of my face tender to touch; my conscience was like typical men. Only I knew what Luca was capable of, "you said my time was up here do you mean that?" Luca looks with confusion his eyes narrowed before saying "I want you so FUCKING bad that you will not be able sit down for weeks after."

It was only then the realization hit us we were delaying the inevitable. "Oh Emily.... Follow me?" I follow with great intensity, knowing once he opened his bedroom door, they were no turning back "Luca stop! I need to tell you something...erm...I'm still a virgin." Luca acted surprised with what I said, then he says "Emily... This is new to me as well," he removes his nicely ironed shirt revealing his torso as he walks over his eyes scanning what was about to happen. He pulls me closer sucking in a deep breath before removing my panties laying me on the soft linen sheets, as he makes his way up the bed kissing my thighs forcing me to scream out, he then stops and for a moment a worrying look came over his face. "Once we do this Emily everything that we have will change," his voice was soft but tender when he spoke before long Luca asked "Are you ready? Tell me to stop if you cannot take no more." He then slowly puts his length inside me making me explode, Luca's breath quickens with every passing moment the feeling is sore, but he slows down, and the pain dissipates and turns to pleasure.

"Fuck that was good..."

As Luca turns over, he notes that I was upset about something, "babe is everything okay?" yes, I grumble knowing that I was not okay, "can we talk Luca? As something has happened, I am needed in London as my only mother has died." "WHAT... oh yeah sure go to London I understand," you could see he was not happy about me going home but why? "Emily! Are you leaving me for good?" "No, my mother has died the family need me with them," Paul took me to London only we were meet by Luca and my brother Danny "WAIT... what are you doing here Luca?"

"That is down to me little sister!" Danny was sweet he always thought about what I wanted, as we walked in the house Danny stopped me. "Little sister I want you to meet the new king," my eyes could not work out why Danny had just said Luca was the new king.

"Danny, a word NOW... What the Fuck Luca is the new king so that makes me his queen yes?"

"Oh, little sister when you stepped down, we had to fined away on getting you back, you might think this is crazy and yeah it is, but this was down to mother not me." Luca looked right at me I turned away mad with what just happened, "Emily I can explain remember Portland I was meeting Danny and your mother. I was going to tell you but then Zofia happened," I took a walk to try and understand what has happened I wanted to go back home and never see the family again.

"Oh, hey Luca ... Can we talk alone?" Luca and I moved away so the family could not interrupt us, "look this was not meant to happen you being king. If Danny had done what mother asked, we would not be in this mess does the family know about your world? Then that is a no."

"Wait... What are you saying Emily?"

"What I am saying is you take on being king we are FUCKING OVER!"

"You want to do this that's fine but know this Emily I know who you was months ago, you was never going to tell me that you was going to be queen." his voice was mad and I wasn't up for fighting with Luca as he walks away he turns back only to see me being sick, "Emily.. Are you pregnant?" I do not answer back making Luca think I was. He sits me down handing me some water "Luca I think I might be pregnant you know; are you mad with me?" Luca books us to go home and sort things out there we told Danny that we were needed back in Seattle, Luca's voice was shaken when asking was I pregnant. In all this time being around him, they are things yet to find out about this guy, we went back to Seattle not wanting to know about if I was pregnant or not while on the way home, I wanted to face the situation and know. Pulling the test from my Gucci small matelassé shoulder bag to see that I was pregnant, "Emily, I want you to know this. Whatever that test is saying that baby does not have me!"

Unknown to how this was now going to play I came out with, "don't worry I am not pregnant." Luca looks on over grasping my hand with a small grin on his face, pulling up at home Luca goes inside while I broke the test up hoping he would not find out. That evening knowing how Luca was about the baby plan B came right in and

That same night that I find out that I was pregnant something was not right, I was experiencing a brown colour within my urine... I paid a little visit to the medical centre to see the doctor and the midwife, the doctor explained that the symptoms that was showing was of an ectopic pregnancy... I then had a scan to see how many weeks I actually was the scan showed seven to eight weeks gone, the doctors were more than happy to let me go home as this baby would not see the morning...

When heading home after seeing the midwife the pain had gotten worse... I had to let nature take its course by the time I had gotten home they was no more baby, I sat weeping for almost an hour after that is when footsteps approached the bedroom door...

"Emily, you awake?"

"Come in.!

"Good you are awake. Emily, I want us to be a family, but do you really want our child, growing up around everything that I stand for?"

"Luca this isn't going to be nice what I am about to tell you, but around 7.30pm tonight I miscarried our baby I am so sorry."

"Hey, don't be I am the one that is sorry!"

It has been about five months since we last saw Zofia, and she was wanting to talk with me "Emily Wait... I know what you must be thinking right now, but I am asking you to not fall in love with Luca that man does not know what love is and as for you I am worried for you Emily. When Luca has gotten what he wants from you he will send you on your way trust me I know firsthand how he is Emily, I know him!"

"Zofia! This is my number call me I want to know more about him," Zofia went on her way she had gotten in my head about Luca or was Luca, right? When Paul sees me, he takes a little step back watching me, but Luca stops him as Luca had some work that needed sorting, "Emily what's wrong?" "Funny you asked that Luca so here something for you? What happened with you and Zofia all of them years ago?"

"I told you Emily you know everything, why ask that?"
"Doesn't Matter why but know this we are OVER!"
"WHAT THE FUCK?"

Chapter 2

"Emily don't walk away from me we can sort this out." Maybe talking with Zofia was the wrong move but looking at Lucas expression gave me what I needed to know, after walking up and down the hallway Luca comes up to me holding his arms out knowing that I would fall into them. I remembered that at that moment I was only a housekeeper, "Hey Emily... Are you okay?" The voice was not Luca's when I looked up and saw Paul standing over me, I wanted to cry, "Emily I have seen how Luca is with you but take this as some friendly advice give it time with Luca." Paul walks away when Luca comes back into the hallway Paul says something to him that makes him grin, "Luca you might not want to talk but know this I AM FUCKING IN LOVE WITH YOU, but we have to stop fighting."

"Emily... Wait when you came here something about you said you was different to any other woman, I know that now, but love isn't something I know that well." At that moment, the door went Luca opens to see a woman that he does not know, "can we help you miss?" The woman looks into Luca's eyes and then says, "hello my only son... Been a long time since you saw me," Luca's eyes widened his nostrils flaring at knowing the woman that abandoned him is standing on his doorstep. "Why are you FUCKING HERE mother?" His voice deepened with every passing moment; he takes his mother by the throat pinning her to the wall before hitting her in the stomach.

He turns round knowing that I was watching, "Emily stop!" I run away locking the door behind me "Emily please come out can we talk about what happened? I reacted without thinking." While in my room trying to figure out what should be done, I pulled my phone out from my back pocket searching for Zofia number, I open the door to find

Luca not standing around what I do see is Paul holding a cup of tea for me. "Is Luca here?" "No, he went out don't know when he will be back," Paul's words made me feel better only Luca's mother was in the house.

I walk down the hall to meet Luca's mother, "you must be Emily? Come sit here," I watch her with great intensity.

Until a voice says "Emily, I want you to meet Caroline... For whatever reason," you could tell that Caroline and Luca had not seen one another since Luca's post adolescence. From what had been said, Caroline had the child when she was 16 years old.

When Caroline was back in college, she met someone called Danny, he was not much older than her at this time, but Caroline loved having the boys chase her. Danny was in his last year at college when Caroline came to Fresh more college, Danny had been known to sleep around. It was after Danny had left the college that Caroline realized she was pregnant, now Caroline know being a single mother was going to be tough, when the child turned 18, he became lost, moving in circles that even the police would avoid and even becoming involved in illegal bare-knuckle fighting.

Caroline had been with us for about a week now, and the more she was around Luca's anxiety levels were through the roof. Caroline had not seen her son since he was 18 years old, Luca wanted her gone, he knows with his mother around that his work could not be done.

"Paul...Emily word NOW!" When Luca called us, we know not to keep him waiting, "now my mother showing up has got people talking around here. So here is what we are going to do, kill her," unknown to us Caroline and Zofia had been meeting up and talking. At that moment when Luca suggested to kill his own mother, I saw then the guy Zofia had told me about, my head was like you need to run away before you are pulled under with what was happening.

How could I love someone like this? I was slowly seeing the man that people had warned me about. I could not stand around knowing all this, my head wanted me to go and tell the police but doing that would only provoke interest. I could not turn to anyone at this moment the person that I so wanted to tell was back in London, when Luca had gone to meet with someone, I headed out hoping that someone would not see me walking around.

Standing outside the place that could save me, suddenly Luca's car caught my eye, lucky for me it was only Paul in the car. Paul pulled up and walked on over to me, "Miss Winters what you are doing here?" "Paul this has to stop someone has to bring him down." His eyes filled with rage but then he says, "do you want me to come in with you?"

"No... This is on me," as I took a step into the unknown, I could not do this without knowing everything. Then I look back to see not only Paul but Zofia as well, Zofia took my hand before saying "we have to do this now Emily."

Walking out knowing that the police now have Luca on their radar. Zofia had told them what she knows only I had backed out telling them, Zofia was now under witness protection. I went back to the house; Paul had a look on his face that was a look of concern. Luca was waiting for us he let me walk past him, but Paul was left lying on the floor covered in his own blood, Luca had seen us going to the police I ran over to help Paul, but Luca took me by my hair and slammed my face into the wall.

Luca walks away leaving me but dragging Paul along the floor, when Luca came back Paul wasn't with him, had he killed the only person that he trusted? That night Luca wanted to talk alone with me, when he had seen what he had done to me his face went into a grin. "Before you say anything to me Emily, I want you to know that Paul has gone," "WHAT THE HELL... Is he okay Luca?"

"Now Emily your face looks sore. I am sorry Emily only you went behind my back," he walks over to me holding his hand out wanting me to take his hand.

The following day as I woke up seeing Luca sleeping, I pulled my phone out to call Danny but then the door opened and standing at the edge of the bed was someone called Smithy.

Chapter 3

Back in the day, Smithy and Luca were good friends and Zofia was the housekeeper. Now Smithy had not been working with Luca that long, but when Smithy sore that Luca had people doing what he wanted Smithy wanted it. Smithy would use Zofia to his every opportunity, Smithy wanted Zofia to fall in love with Luca so he could take over.

We went into the hallway, so we did not wake Luca up. "You missed me, Emily?" "Why now Smithy what we had was something special, but remember you made Zofia go mad." Smithy had been a friend to me back in high school, "Emily... Luca needs to know he can't do what he does to people." When Luca woke up and saw Smithy, he looked really pissed. "what's it been Luca ten years since you last seen me and here, I am, back to get what's owed to me," "FUCK YOU!"

Emily walks back into the bedroom. Knowing that Luca was not to be crossed I headed into the bedroom keeping the door open, "so Smithy you want what is owed? Take it and yes, I know back then you were seeing Emily."

"Oh, Caroline nice to see your thanks for telling me you were here, should we now tell Luca what we have be hiding all this time."

"WHAT... what have you been hiding all this time?"

I enter out the room to be told that Smithy was Luca's brother, "you look shocked Luca anything to say?" he turns away trying to work this out. "Luca how did you know about me all of them years ago?"

"Smithy told me about you that's why Emily..." Smithy and Caroline turned and walked out the door leaving Luca filled with anger, "Luca what's going on?"

"Nothing Emily don't talk to me..."

After the revelation that Smithy was Luca's brother, the mood had not improved Caroline and Smithy were more than likely far away from here now. Luca had gone before I wake up, he went looking for Smithy and Caroline because Luca was out my cell phone went. I answered the phone, and the voice was Paul, "Emily come and meet with me alone you need to know something." Luca had been asking people to keep an eye open if they saw Smithy and Caroline to call him, I was about to head out when the door opened Luca was covered in blood and threw Smithy to the floor.

"Luca! Stop he is your brother..."

"Emily FUCK YOU he will die NOW."

Luca pulls out the gun that I never knew he had, as he was about to shoot Smithy, I step in the way making Luca drop the gun. As Smithy lays on the floor covered in his own blood, I turn to Luca his eyes narrowed his attention fully on Smithy. In that second Luca looks at me his eyes soften, "Luca let this go what ever happened has happened you really want to keep living in the past."

I helped Smithy up from the floor with Luca looking on and for once he does something nice, he calls for help when the medic's came Smithy says. "He was hit by a car covering up what Luca had done," Luca whispers "thank you."

Luca heads to court over what happened with Zofia. Out the blue Luca decides to plead guilty her family are taken back when he says it, Luca know pleading not guilty would send it to a trial the judge takes what Luca had pleaded and passed an 18-month suspended sentence. As he walks out the court room Zofia comes over and says, "WE'RE DONE NOW." I headed back to London to see Danny as he was about to be coronated as King, Danny only took being king on as Luca had said no to being king when back in London, I remembered that this was my home.

When in London I met someone that was nothing like the man I am with. I was broken inside Luca had pulled me under and I did not want that with a man, when the man said who he was it came as a shock to me it was Paul.

As time went on Paul and I were getting closer and closer, since being back in London I had not spoken to Luca he was like a memory. Knowing the trip to London was ending and having to see Luca once more I was feeling strong to cope with the trouble, he has following him. Something was telling me not to go back but Luca keep calling me, as I went back to Seattle Luca was there to meet me, he put his arms around me and said, "Had a nice time away?" Being back with Luca I know what I needed to do to keep him on side, as he opened the car door for me his eyes filled with rage but when I asked, "what was wrong?" His eyes softened a little on the journey home the car was filled with deadly silent apart from the soft drumming of the radio.

As we pulled up outside home Luca turns to me. "Don't ever go away without running it past me you are mine Emily, and why you are with me it's my duty to keep you safe!"

That night went slow as Luca headed to bed the doorbell went. He opens the door to see Paul with Smithy, Smithy walks in hugging his brother but Lucas eyes was locked onto Paul. "Brother let Paul say what he has to say?" "You have five seconds to explain!" As Paul spoke Luca got increasingly frustrated but then Luca holds his hand out to Paul, Luca turns to me Paul and Smithy left, his eyes filled with anger Luca then takes my chin and lays a sweet kiss on my lips.

The bedroom is like I remember, he lay my naked body on the soft bedding, as Luca removes the boxers showing his length, we gazed into each other's eyes for a moment a moment that felt like an eternity. We made love a fell into a deep sleep in each other's arms. Luca woke up at 3.30am and headed to his office I could hear him pacing up and down.

Chapter 4

I wake to find a note from Luca it says, "back in five days from now," with Luca gone leaving me alone I keep thinking what happens if someone needs him. Luca had gone back to the place that he went to when he was a kid that was New York City, he needed to find that boy that he once was I could not be in the house alone, so I went to fined him. As I got into New York Luca was waiting for me his face went into a small grin, "Hey. You what you cannot be without me Miss Winters?" "Don't call me that you know my name." As we walked back to what Luca calls a second home he stops and turns to me, "Miss Winters sorry Emily would you MARRY ME?"

It took me back a little when he asked me then I replied "YES! On one condition that is you will not go mad when I tell you that I am pregnant again," his eyes narrowed he was about to say something then replied with "this is so mad but it's what I want with you Emily." What came more as a shock was when Luca told me that Paul was here with us, Paul had made things right with Luca what they did not tell me was Luca always made people think before they crossed him.

Luca wanted us to be married before we went back to Seattle. "Luca Hunny ... can we have the wedding in London? Or we can get married here and then have one in London?" Lucas eyes rolled before he said, "why can't I ever say no to you Miss Winters," joking around with what looked to be like he is finely exploring love. Why in New York Luca got news about who his father was all Luca was told about him was he wanted to meet him, his father was called Edison Luke Lavigne he had so many questions that needed to be answered from Edison. On the last night in New York Edison meet with his son, for a moment Luca was hostile to him but softened when Edison spoke, Edison told Luca that his mother Caroline was wanting him out the house before they adopted Luca.

All of them years Luca was told a boy called Danny was his father, Luca wanted to meet with his mother, but Caroline had not been seen in a while.

As we got back into Seattle, we were welcomed by someone. This person knows Luca and what he had been doing, they wanted to know answers that only Luca alongside Paul know. It was when they said that they were an old housekeeper that Lucas eyes filled with anger, when I know Paul and Luca had them under control that is when I went to the car. I could see that the woman was upset on how Luca went about his activities with all this happening could we get married without trouble? When I spotted Paul walking to the car alone my head was like no Luca what has happened? Moments after Luca followed his eyes raging with anger his eyes soften when they meet with mine, on the way home Luca and Paul was talking about this woman but gave no name to her.

The woman had put Luca on the edge but since the woman has shown up, Paul has taken some time away it came to my attention that Luca and this woman had history. Going back to when we came home from New York the woman said something about a child, now that is when I went back to the car, I never gave it consideration but now it is playing on my mind.

I headed into the living room to fined Luca watching a film the film he was watching everyone know. I sat to one side looked over at Luca and said, "really ROCKY?" Luca smirks back at me his eyes not moving from the film it took me a while to think what one he was watching, then when I saw MR T it was obvious ROCKY 3, I remember when I met Luca, he said ROCKY was his go to film. Watching the film, you know that ROCKY would win back his championship, once it ended Luca looked at me to see me sleeping, he carried me into the bedroom.

I wake to find myself not in my bed but Luca's bed I fell right back to sleep. That morning at the breakfast bar Lucas eyes meets with mine, he grins then heads to the door as I turn to see Danny it was nice to see him, but Luca needed to talk with him. "Danny... I wanted to ask you something could I have Emily's hand in marriage?" Before Danny answers him Danny notices that I am pregnant he looks back at Luca and says, "this isn't happening your answer is NO!" The mood becomes toxic Lucas eyes become dark and filled with anger, "as the king and with my little sister pregnant with your child I hereby claim your child as a BASTARD."

"Oh, I almost forgot. If this wedding happens, I will behead Luca, and due to this Emily, your child will not be known as a prince or princess." Danny then walks out the door leaving us unknown of what to do, Luca turns to me his face filled with disappointment, Luca wanted to go after Danny, but Paul stopped him Luca's anger got the better of him. After lashing out at me Luca headed out oh ready having drunk·a full bottle of scotch, the following day Luca came home his mood was still the same. Knowing the mood Luca was in I locked my room door, once I know Luca had passed out, I pulled out my phone to call Smithy lucky he was in Seattle, so he came on over to see what had happened.

Luca's drinking had become increasingly frequent, thanks to Paul and Smithy they got Luca away from the drinking. As we headed to New York for the wedding Danny called me to inform me that the wedding now had his blessing, only Smithy and Paul came to the wedding as the minister said we was now husband and wife I looked over to see Danny. "Little sister... Now you are married to Luca you understand that Luca must now die," "FUCK

YOU ASS HOLE." Danny took a step back looked over at Luca and said, "your time will come before long," Luca took my hand to show Danny that he did not bother us we walked by him.

"STOP NOW......If Luca doesn't die then your child will!"

Luca turns to face Danny... Danny's eyes was cold like ice showing no emotion Smithy takes me to the car why Danny and Luca talk, Luca and Danny came to an agreement the agreement was as followed and that was Luca had to hand himself over to the police or die. As we made it home Luca opened another bottle of scotch what was meant to a joyful day turned to sour grapes, I went to talk to him, but his mood told me what I needed to know. The Luca I know would fight but now he turns to the bottle Paul and Smithy was taking on Luca's work now, Danny had gotten to Luca I wanted to help my husband, but I was unsure on what could help him.

"Luca...Hunny do you want to talk about it?"

"No... NO FUCK OFF."

"Don't talk to Emily like that," as Luca tried to stand, he fell right back down Smithy checked to see if I was okay, I nodded to say, "fine thanks." After Luca had got rid of Danny out his head and looked at what he had been putting away, he turns to me and says "Emily... Would sorry cut it this time?" his eyes met with mine before we shared a kiss with each other, I couldn't work out weather Luca had become a new man or had love really taken over him? I know that Luca was trying to give up what he had done for years but it came with challenges, Luca got news that the woman that wanted answers was back in Seattle Paul and Smithy went with Luca to see what she wanted.

Chapter 5

When Luca was with the woman, he came to understand that people do not forget. Smithy and Paul watched from two table's away, Luca wanted to know about the child but the woman changing moving the conversation away from the child. Luca became increasingly frustrated with the woman that is when she told him what her name was her name was Naomi, he looked into her eyes and then know that Naomi was someone that he did love once. Naomi worked for Luca when he was 18 years old Luca looks over at Paul and Smithy as to ask, "WHAT NOW," Luca turns back to Naomi and says, "the child is mine?" She grins then stands up and says, "see you around Luca!" When they came back from the meeting Luca looks at Smithy and Paul as to say, "leave us... Emily can we talk?"

"Emily, you know how much I love you don't you? The woman I met with today her name is Naomi she is the mother to my child that I never knew about." "Luca why are you saying this now? Every time we fined away to move on someone or something else turns up, we have only been married days I need time to understand this I am going to my room."

I so wanted to run away. But now that Luca and I were married I hoped that he would now open up more than what he has done, "Smithy what mood is Luca in?" He looked into my eyes and went "Emily my brother is your problem now," I turn round only to be met by my husband his eyes filled with anger as I was about to talk Luca stops me. "Emily my dear wife... You look upset do you want to talk? I want be mad with whatever you ask," unsure on what Luca would do we went for dinner that is when I asked has, he met his child?

Lucas eyes rolled when I asked the question but answered with "Not as yet..." Luca ordered Paul to keep watch on what Naomi did, in that moment the door opened it was Edison he had come to see Luca about his mother Caroline. Edison had come to tell us that Caroline had been to see him "Edison... I need you to tell me is Caroline heading this way, Luca wants to kill her that is why I am asking?"

Luca looked into Edison's eyes I took a step back unsure on what Luca would do, that is when Luca put his hand out for Edison to shake. Edison does not shake his sons hand you could see the anger boiling up in Lucas eyes when Edison did not shake his hand, "You know Edison... You might be my father, but the apple does not fall far from the tree." As we got home, we were welcomed by Caroline, "NOW WHAT Caroline?" you haven't been seen for months and here you are in my Fucking home," Luca turns to me before asking me to head to our room. "Well Caroline... Or should I say mother, you have two choices leave now or die?" Caroline was here to put things right with Luca, as Caroline turned to Smithy a shot was fired, had Caroline or Smithy been shot.

The gun shot had missed Smithy and had hit Caroline killing her out right... I turned to see Emily holding the gun, Smithy stood back up only to see Emily had fired the gun once the smoke had cleared, I took Emily out the room. "Luca I'm so sorry it wasn't supposed to kill anyone what happens now?" "Emily do what I say stay here and let me and Smithy deal with this SHIT," Smithy and Paul took the body from the house whilst I sorted Emily out.

When I went back to Emily, she had become a broken mess... I gave Edison a call and told him what Emily had done, as her husband I picked her up from the floor reassuring Emily that she will not go down for this, but her eyes said something else. As Paul and Smithy came back to the house Emily was sleeping in her room why Smithy said, "well what was the reason behind her killing Caroline?" I came out with "she was protecting us and the baby," Paul lent over and said, "sir, do you want me to take Emily away from here?" I replied "NO... Emily stays here with me for now."

Following the events with me killing Caroline the only thing worrying me was law enforcement breaking down the door to arrest me. Days went by and the only person around was Luca. Smithy and Paul had been sent to find out more about this Naomi, it was then that Naomi showed up at the house. Once Paul and Smithy came back my mind was put at rest but when Paul and Smithy know that Naomi was talking to Luca, Naomi had told Luca that she wanted him to meet the child.

"Thanks for coming Naomi..."

"No problem bye Luca..."

Luca turned and looked right at me he knew there was a problem, only the look he gave me was like talk when we are alone. News broke that some human remains had been found the police wanted to find out the name before they said any more, people had been guessing that it could be local high school student that went missing years ago. It turned out that the body was Caroline's when Luca got the news, he put the house into lock-down, Luca did not want me talking to the police he got Paul to take me to New York knowing the police would come at some point in time.

Once people know the remains was Lucas's mother the spotlight came right on to us... Smithy had removed the gun that I shot Caroline with, the police spoke with Luca about when he last saw his mother the detective wanted to now talk with me. I made up a story that Caroline came her months ago and that was the last we had seen her, when the detective arrested Smithy on the murder, I looked at Luca only to see him laughing that he had set his own brother up.

As they took Smithy away, I placed my hand over my baby bump, asking myself could my child be Smithy's.

As night falls the house is filled with anger over what Luca had done... I wanted to ask my husband why but when I spotted him talking with Paul I walked away, leaving them talking my cell phone rang it was an unknown number I answered. "Emily are you alone?"

"Yes why?"

"I will go down for this, keep our child away from him..."
"My child will only know one person as the dad and that is Luca bye Smithy."

Chapter 6

Smithy was charged with manslaughter... He pleaded guilty to that but not guilty to murder the case would now await a trial date, Smithy would now be holed in police custody Luca know with Smithy doing time that he would now be able to work without any bother. Once Edison had been told that Smithy was up on a manslaughter charge Edison came to see Luca about this, even with Smithy not being biological to Edison always made sure Smithy got the help as well. Smithy biological father went missing before he was even born, "Edison nice to see you again... What you want me to tell the police that my own wife killed Caroline?" The answer is "NO... So, FUCK YOU!"

"Do not walk away from me Luca... I'm here to help you for whatever reason you might have not to listen but will, you will help Smithy walk free or I tell them it was Emily..." Luca turns to Edison his eyes now raging with anger but then Paul stops what was about to happen, Edison walks out the door looking at me as to say Luca must do the right thing.

Edison knows with putting Lucas back to the wall that Luca would act out before long... When Edison was about 15 years old, Edison was sent down for a remarkably similar case that Smithy is facing Edison was going to prove that Smithy did not kill Caroline. Edison knows by threatening Luca that Luca would more than likely want to talk again, Edison had fined away to keep me from going down and to make Smithy a free man, but he needed Luca to agree that was going to be impossible. After Luca had gotten me alone, he sat me down and asked, "do you think Edison will get Smithy walking free?" In that moment I came out with "dear husband only you can sort this not me."

Knowing deep down that it was me that could put a stop to all this... Once Smithy's trial got under way, we could not even move for people wanting to talk with us, the trial went on for about five weeks all we were now waiting on is the verdict. Then Edison made the move that Luca never seen coming Edison had given the police some information that got Smithy walking free, the added information that Edison gave showed that Smithy had been set up. Lucky Edison had not given them my name he told them that it was his only son Luca,

when the police re questioned Luca somehow, he walked away for now... The investigating officer wanted to talk with everyone again, for some reason or another Luca know not to cross Edison more than once as Edison made it clear that he would not only take me down but Luca as well. The investigating officer had now re questioned everyone, and then made that Caroline's killing was done accidental what Edison keep away from Luca was that he was working with an undercover agent.

The time had come for Luca to meet his unknown child... Luca was not sure on what to do thanks to me talking with Naomi she was happy for me to go with Luca, when Luca met his son, he realised that his son was severely ill with an exceedingly rare condition. "Luca are you okay?" He turns to Naomi with tears rolling down his face I had never seen Luca cry before like I have now, "why didn't you say something Naomi? I have missed so many years with this little man." Luca gave Naomi some money for his ill son, but Naomi was not too keen on taking the money in till Luca said his son needs it more, Luca gave Naomi over $2.5 million to make sure his son got the best treatment. For Luca that was like giving money to a homeless person then making it back with the work he does, as we made it home, we were welcomed by Edison and Smithy...

"Brother... What do you need now from me?" They had come to talk about Smithy working alongside me only Edison went onto say see this as compensation, when Edison said that I know this was for setting Smithy up about killing Caroline. "Luca you would do well to remember I want only take Emily down, but I would also take you down as well," "FUCK YOU EDISON!"

"Give him time Smithy and when the time is right then we move in for the kill..." "But when will that be? We have worked on this case now for over two years," "I know just a little longer what I need from you is get Emily on side..."

"I can't keep acting as his brother and you can't keep up the daddy act..." Knowing that we were about to bring down a man that will never see the outside again, was exciting once we had the evidence to give to the CPS, we could then sleep easy at night. We had been to see Danny to tell him that Emily would be keep safe when we finely arrest Luca Lavigne, back in 2019 a case came into the office the case was as followed it said that we were dealing with an excessively big drug dealer.

The case needed people to get on the inside. We know when the case came in that Smithy would be able to find out trivial things from Emily as they have history, so leading up to us going in we had to have a plan, so we know Smithy and Caroline was good mates. Caroline agreed to find her son we know Caroline could make Luca understand that Smithy was his brother, once Caroline had gotten Luca to see that Smithy was his brother, we know then we were in. Me on the other hand I know that it would take longer than it did with Smithy, that is when I had to write a letter saying that I was Luca's father we know that Luca would have questions, and he did as well.

We know that it was not going to be as straightforward as what we had made out... Once Luca know that he could trust Smithy he ended up showing all his suppliers, then once we had them, we sent people to follow them. After

Caroline died and Luca had set Smithy up, we know that Luca was working things out that is why we backed away a little but keep people on the inside, when Smithy told us that Luca was married to Emily, we had to then work out how we could keep Emily safe.

What we did not know was when Zofia came to us about what Luca had done to her... The evidence that Zofia gave us about him, made us investigate Luca even more we find that Luca had over 18 house keepers that was not including Emily.

I turned Luca his eyes are filled with anger yet again... Luca cups my chin before laying a passionate kiss on me when Smithy came walking in the door, he sees us kissing and walks by us you know Smithy could not let me be happy with Luca... "Emily now we are on our own I want you to know something, I am not Lucas brother and Edison isn't Lucas father."

"WHAT... Why are you saying this, Smithy?"

"I want to tell you everything but now isn't the time..."

Smithy's news came as a shock, but I could not help thinking does Luca know. Edison and Smithy meet with the CPS, they told them that everything they have was not that strong Edison then know that he needed to turn up the pressure.

Chapter 7

Even now married to the woman that walked into my life as the housekeeper. I know that then something had to give but now I am unsure on what to say, this story was not to end with me married to her I never wanted Emily to know about what I am. The night when Emily killed my mother, I know then that Emily was the same and now we are about to welcome our child, this world that I am stuck in is not for a woman like Emily I should set her free, but she knows too much. I sat watching Emily sleeping before my attention was broken with Edison talking to Smithy, "boss guess what? We have news and you will want to know this follow us into the meeting room..." Waking up to find the room empty was a blessing knowing that Smithy is talking with Luca gave me time to think, unsure if Luca know about Edison and Smithy I got dressed and headed out the house...

Why out walking I went into the book shop... I need to know why they wanted to put Luca away the archives had a story on Luca dating back some time ago, the story they had was about a woman not much older than what I am her name was? But once I read some more about this woman and why Luca killed her that was when I took myself back to when Zofia was about, the woman that Luca killed was Zofia younger sister...

The only person that would really understand would be Danny in some way, after getting home Edison had gone but Smithy was sat in the living room alone... Luca had gone to meet with a new supplier I wasn't wanting to talk with Smithy, but he wanted to talk, about how long Edison and himself had long left on Luca they was closing in on him..

"Hey Luca, you got a moment? We need to talk as husband and wife..." Knowing Smithy was in the house we got Paul to take him out why I talked with Luca, "they are no other way on telling you Luca Smithy and Edison are police, and they are closing in on you." "What? Are you saying Edison is not my father and Smithy is not my brother?" Luca eyes rage with anger he was going red in the face, Luca then headed out leaving me alone in the house...

"Hey is Luca about?"

"Sorry Smithy, you missed him he knows everything," "Emily why tells him?" I do not answer back on why Smithy then calls Edison to let him know that Lucas onto them. Paul heads out looking for Luca Smithy and Edison are now angry that Luca knows, when Luca walks in the door his mood had not changed, he then tells Paul to get new locks for the house. Luca then calls the people he knows and tells them to keep low they don't even ask why? He then turns to me and asked, "how long have you known about them?" I replied, "some weeks now I'm sorry," Lucas eyes darken about me knowing before him when Paul came back with the new locks Edison followed him into the house...

Luca took Edison by the throat pinning him to the wall... Lucas eyes fill with pure anger before armed police came running in the house, while the police had Luca on the floor they conducted a house search they never find any drugs or suspicious money laying around... Luca had been doing this since he was 18 years old so he know what they would look fore, they took Luca for questioning and put the house under surveillance watch... Why Luca was locked up Paul had been planning his and Luca's escape, that is when I wondered was, I going with them?

The police know that questioning Luca that he would only cooperate with them, if they gave him what he wanted Luca to know how to manipulate the system... They handed Luca something to think about they offered him a deal, they wanted names times and dates for his freedom Luca looked at them and laughed the offer away he was not wanting to cooperate...

After days in questioning and not cooperating they let Luca Walk free.... He walked back in the door confident as ever, only to be meet with an angry pregnant wife that wanted to know why her husband was going on the run without her? "Emily you are weeks away from having baby, that is why the team has not involved you... So when the police do come looking for me you want none the wiser to my whereabouts that is why we have not involved you..." Luca then cups my chin laying a passionate kiss to my forehead before Paul calls him away, "Edison come and sit down we need to talk, when I gave you this case I wanted answers not more questions... Edison you have gave me no choice but to remove you from the case as you have royally FUCKED THIS UP," Smithy would now work alongside Detective Marsden now that Marsden was running this he called a meeting with Smithy...

"Smithy, I want you to get back on the inside... Who knows what is going on right now? So, call Luca and get his trust back now!" Against Lucas better judgement he let Smithy back in the house, in what every case Marsden has worked on in the end he always gets the conviction... Marsden's win loss record was clean Marsden had over 1000 people convicted, he had never loss, yet you could say Marsden always got his case done before it was needed to be done...

"Mr Lavigne thanks for coming, I'm Detective Marsden do you have time to answer some questions?" Luca moves uncomfortably knowing Marsden was not intimidated by him, each question Marsden asked Luca became increasingly frustrated. As Marsden sat back looking right into Lucas eyes Marsden grins before letting Luca go, "now that is how you need to be Edison" Marsden's comment angered Edison more than it should have done...

"Are you okay? Luca what did they say to you?"

"Take me home now Paul and don't ask questions you got that?"

"Yes sir..."

Marsden then orders Smithy to find out everything about Luca right down to his shoe size... Marsden had looked at how Caroline was killed, Marsden spotted that Luca had covered up that it was Emily that killed Caroline and that it was no accident... After Luca came home from the police, he told me to pack a bag for him and myself, unsure on what was going on I did as I was told that is when Paul came to the room and said "Marsden has your husband's number..."

Luca began moving money about in case Marsden went looking round the accounts... "Luca nice to see you again if you don't mind, we would like to re question you, about the night your mother Caroline was killed down at the station." Paul followed them down with Lucas legal team behind him, once in the interview room Marsden then reads Luca his rights...

After Marsden had questioned Luca on the events, Marsden went to the cps with the evidence they looked and nodded at Marsden this time Luca was not coming home... The police now had Luca on perverting the course of justice and when they looked at the bank accounts, they also had him on money laundering Luca was now feeling the pressure... Luca asked Marsden for a moment with the legal team once they was alone Luca turns to his team and said "I'm paying you Fucking good money and you are doing nothing," that is when Marsden came back into the room and let Luca go pending further investigation....

Now Luca was alone with Smithy he then turns to Smithy and asked, "weather he could get onto the database?" Smithy knows hacking the database could only mean one thing, Luca wanted Smithy to remove his case so that he could be a free man...

Chapter 8

"Hey... Luca do you have time to talk? There is something I need to tell you as a matter of urgency, and what I must tell you might come as some interest not only to you but Emily as well." Luca answers with "not now but later," I watch him walk out the door knowing that the news could really send him over the edge... I wanted to be a 100% sure that Luca was adopted, so when the evidence came back to me that Caroline and Edison wasn't his biological parents all that was needed was to tell Emily and Luca, I made sure that Edison was here knowing Luca was going to fucking kill me for having Edison in the house... Lucas biological parents died about two years ago all I knew was the surname was Hamilton, that also came with other news I was Lucas biological brother so when Luca walked in the door with Emily and spotted Edison tempers flared...

"Luca I can explain let's sit down and talk?"

"I was wanting to tell you this earlier, but you said later so here it goes, you were called Hamilton up until you turned five, yes?"

"GET TO THE POINT!"

"Okay Luca you was adopted when you turned five years old, the reason Edison is here is to tell you that is because it's not a lie and that I am infect your brother..." Luca stands up his eyes filled with anger and his nostrils flaring he was about to lose his shit, until I gave him the evidence he then turns to Emily ordering her to leave the room... Luca goes to speak but stops then turns to Edison and asked "was you really going to put your own son in prison?"

"Luca, I was working a case I did not know it was you until we met in New York... If I knew then that it was you, I would not have taken the case on," Luca then turns his attention back to me before asking "why make out you was family?" I go to answer, but Luca stops me yet again before he yells out "FUCK THIS SHIT," slamming his fist into the wall cutting his hand open "I want a DNA done on you Smithy to make sure you are not lying to me..."

Luca then ordered me to check on Emily because while he spoke with Edison... I stand outside the door waiting to see whether the talk would turn into a fight, but it does not, Emily spots me standing in the hallway she goes to ask something, but I do not let her talk knowing Edison and Luca was in the room behind, us we move away then I let her talk...

We headed into the kitchen that is when Luca barks an order, we stop dead thinking was the order for one of us to answer to... We turn to see Edison he is shifting erratically unknown to us Luca had been told that his son has motor neurone disease, MND affects up to 5,000 adults in the United Kingdom at any one-time, Luca wanted to see his son... While Luca was away, Smithy took the DNA test that Luca wanted him to have done, that evening while I was alone in the house a woman showed up it was Zofia, we had not seen her in so long that she looked different...

"No need to call anyone Emily.... Look when we last spoke, I was upset but the real reason I am here is to ask you something?" "Emily can you really give Luca what he wants? You do not know him like I know him he only married you to stop me from loving him again..."

"You are more delusional than what my husband thinks you are!!"

"I am not fucking delusional Emily.... You know we was friends but since you married that asshole you really became one fucking BITCH drop dead," the door slams as Zofia walks away before Smithy asked was that...? I cut him off before he says any more... Once Luca came home after seeing his son, Smithy gives him the test results and there in black and white, showing that Smithy was blood, Lucas eyes darken more than usually before he says....

"Smithy what do you know about the Hamilton's?" In that second, my eras prick up at the name Hamilton unsure if not to say something, "the Hamilton name is legendary they were the ones that founded the monarchy."

"It looks like your wife knows more about our family then we do BROTHER!"

"Leave Emily alone Smithy...If my wife has something to say then let her talk, right?" Smithy then walks away while Edison is still standing in the hallway, the Hamilton family owned most houses around the London area that is when Luca wanted to know more.... Luca pulled his macbook out and looked up the name Hamilton and that came with challenges on its own, the Hamilton family are in line to take the throne as members have married into our weird family....

After spending time finding out about the Hamilton family, we also find out that by rights Danny was not meant to be king... The line of succession does not show that we were meant to take the throne, we looked again, and the throne should have gone to a Hamilton...

Chapter 9

I couldn't understand why the next person to the throne was a Hamilton... Mother when she was alive said that the throne went to me or Danny, this now means that Danny would have to abdicate being king so that a Hamilton could take the throne... Luca did find out that when he was a Hamilton he was 8th in line to be king, and after Luca it would be passed on to Smithy then it would be me then Danny in the line of succession.... Once we had worked the succession line out Luca's phone rang, he gotten news that his son had passed away....

"WHAT... You do not want me at the hospital?"

Luca's voice was becoming frustrated with Naomi I could understand in a way, then on the other hand I remembered what Luca had told me about her.... Naomi knows how to make Lucas blood boil and what made it more frustrating, was that Naomi played the single mother act that is when Luca sent Smithy to her house to find out why she wanted nothing more from Luca...

Unknown to us our problems were about to become a lot more serious... Nothing goes to plan when you are married to a man that is so always looking for his next hit, that was not what was on my mind, what was on my mind was that Danny was about to be removed from being king... The Hamilton family now had the person that was set to take on being king, and when Danny was told that he had to step down as king the blame came right at me and Luca like it was us that had him removed... With in days off Danny finding out he was being removed I got an incredibly angry letter from Danny, of course Danny expresses that mother would not allow her baby boy to be removed as king...

"Emily... It seems like Danny has gotten the news about him being removed as king, I have just had a long talk with Danny he is one pissed man..."

"Fuck... Luca are you okay?"

"Yeah, nothing Danny says really bothers me...."

As Luca is about to walk away from me, Detective Marsden turned back up with other officers, Marsden must have been expecting trouble.... Luca doesn't even fight back when Marsden reads him his rights I'm taken back when Luca goes with Marsden quietly, once down at the station Marsden formally charges Luca on a number of things... Luca would now wait on a court date with no police bail, thanks to Luca being organised I know what to do with the house, the police went through the house with a fine tooth comb and took the mac-books that Luca owned....

Marsden had waited five years to have Luca Lavine locked away, the news was that Marsden would retire after this case....

Smithy and Edison were then called to be questioned by Marsden.... That is when people find out that it was me that killed Caroline, thanks to Detective Marsden he made the Caroline shooting go away it was not me he was wanting it was my husband and he had him now.... Unknown to me Marsden worked it that Luca would only be doing up to ten to fifteen years inside, this was down to something that only Marsden and Luca knew about....

The Hamilton family timeline is difficult to understand... As we know Smithy and Luca are Hamilton's even though Luca now goes under the Levine name, he took the Lavine name at the ages off 10 years old due to Caroline not wanting him to have the Hamilton name.... Now with Marsden he is a Hamilton right down to the point, the Hamilton name dates to the Nineteen Hundreds as the records show us.... Knowing what we do about the Hamilton's the person that would take over from Danny would be Marsden, after moving out the house Smithy kindly let me move in with him......

But when Paul asked what about him Smithy left Paul out in the cold.... Like he was nothing Smithy had done something that Luca would not dream about doing, to Luca, Paul was his trusted assistant. I was not happy with Smithy for leaving Paul out in the cold.... It was like Smithy had become the new Luca overnight, but in an unusual way whatever Smithy did he did alone with no trusted assistants at his side...

While unpacking in the small room, Smithy had kindly made into a bedroom I came across something that had our child's name on... "Emily I won't be long something has come up, are you needing anything before I head out?" I open the door and answer with "what happens if I need anything?" Smithy answers back with "well that is why you have a phone Emily," I open the box to find money and what looked like a letter from Luca...

Once Smithy had come home, he asked "Emily why has Luca sent you a letter wanting to see you? You know Emily he is not allowed to even talk to you never mind seeing you...

Chapter 10

As morning breaks, I wake to find a letter asking me to give evidence against Luca... Sending what was a nice morning into nothing but worry, had I not walked into Luca's life I would now be the queen, in that second all my emotions came rushing out... Smithy mood had become more approachable, he had also had the same letter that I had gotten, "Emily, was you wanting to visit your husband?" The mood in the room shifted but I soon got over it... While Smithy was here, we went back to the house that once was home, but the house had become nothing since I moved out...

On the morning of the trial Smithy lent on over and spoke "you got this Emily," the court room was packed with people watching on from the gallery... As Luca appeared he was having to be helped by the officers, people in the gallery began whispering on what could have happened to him... The jury took their place, and as the judge took his place the opening statements was given... Luca's team argued that Mr Lavine was pushed into this situation, given him no choice but to agree, I looked on over at Smithy shaking his head on what Luca's team was saying....

His team would at every opportunity remind the court, that Luca spent a lot of time in and out of care then they called Zofia to the stand... Her brown eyes met with mine up in the gallery; while being questioned from Luca's team you see Zofia getting herself muddled up... After they questioned her, they turned back to the court and said, "doesn't that prove what this court needs to know?" The prosecution then made the court listen to several 911 calls, that was made when Zofia was working for Luca as the housekeeper...

It was then Paul's turn in the stand, the prosecution showed photos of what Luca had done to Paul of course Luca's team asked the judge does the court need to see this? Luca's team was now scrambling to find something to make the court see that Luca was innocent, you could tell Luca was pissed with his team and what they were doing... The judge then adjourned till 10am the following morning,

"Hey Emily, do not worry its only day one..."

"Thanks Smithy but that won't help me right now..."

The next morning back at court Luca's team, would then tell the court that everything Luca did was nothing like the prosecution was making it out to be.... They then went on to tell the court that Luca was not mentally stable to be here, and it was best interest that the court was adjourned till they manage to sort Luca out... The judge then looked at Luca with people chattering in the gallery, and informed the court to carry on, "may I remind Mr Lavine team that this was a court of law and not some playground..."

"Would it be fair to say Mr Osborne, that my client never made any rational decisions with thinking them over or talking with you? Because was you not my client's trusted assistant in all the time you were working for him?" Paul began sweating with the question before he answered with, "Luca knew how to make people fall in line with him, because of his manipulation techniques... He had full control on everything he did, we were nothing but his puppets," "how can you stand there and represent someone like him? You make everyone that fell victim sick..."

"ENOUGH, remove Mr Osborne from the court now... members of the jury ignore that last remark that was made by Mr Osborne,"

After Paul was removed from the court, Lucas eyes widened, and a sick smile came over his face he turned to the gallery and his eyes met with mine.... I tried not to look but his eyes drew me in that is when the sick fucker blow me a kiss, he knows that blowing me a kiss would more than likely get a reaction from me but unfortunately for him he did not.... After two hours in the court, I managed to chat with Paul about what happened in the court room, "Emily what I said in court was only because his team had gotten to me, I know he's your husband..." The reason Paul gave was good enough for me before I answered back, "Paul I am your friend and always will be...."

In that second, a moment came over us, unknown to us Smithy had seen us kiss we knew then that someone had seen us but who we did not know....

Given what had happened with me and Paul while outside the court, we looked at each other and was unsure whether we should say something... But then we thought what the fuck and we kissed again; this time Paul did not hold back with the kiss.... Paul's rough tongue grazed over my lips sending emotions sky high, before he said, "Emily I have been fighting my feelings for you all this time...." My eyes light up at the words Paul said, I then thought why he has been hiding this, but I was not wanting to break this moment until Paul said, "say something?" Unsure on what to answer back with I said, "how about a cuppa tea and talk about this....

"Emily, I don't drink tea but coffee yes please...." We got our drinks and took a table near the window; we both smiled and then spoke about what happened.... We were like school children, but the world we were in right now was about to be crumbled... When Smithy came walking in the café, "Emily are you okay? Oh, Paul what a surprise or not when was you going to tell me?"

"Smithy what are you on about? Because Paul and I was just talking about court," his eyes narrowed on me and Paul holding hands.... You could see Smithy, burning a hole into Paul until I said, "Smithy it's time we were going...." The closing statements was then given, from the defence team and the prosecution... It took the jury, three weeks to come back with a verdict... The gallery and outside court were

waiting with anticipation as the jury delivered the verdict....
Luca's face dropped from a sick smile to a look off
disappointment when he was found guilty...

Chapter 11

Somehow a tear rolled down my cheek I was unsure why a tear had escaped me, I put it down to my eyes watering but them around me know the real reason why... Luca had become frustrated with how the court had found him guilty, the sentencing came within seconds he was sentenced Luca for everyone he had killed or harmed rounding up everything he had done Luca was given the death sentence... Luca would eventually sit in the electric chair, but something inside told me do you want your own child growing up not knowing his father One day I would need to answer the question? But now what I needed was a mug off tea and something hot inside off me, I so wanted to feast on a Chinese and forget the name Lavine...

Sometime after court Luca's team reopened his case for an appeal... They had managed to find something that had not been looked at with a careful eye, that is when Luca's representative bought this to the attention of the police... Weeks later the new investigator reopened this case and wanted to question people again, it turned out when Luca was questioned the last time nothing had gone on the record.. The police wanted a mental health assessment done on Mr Lavine before carrying out any questioning, they made people give new statements and then compared them to the old statements... Lieutenant Swain looked at the relationship that had happened with Emily and Luca's pass relationships to see whether they were any consistency with them, after spending time on the case Swain stated that it should had never gone to trial... Swain pulled up Luca's family and medical history and that is when the penny dropped for her, Swain then called a meeting with her team and her boss to explain the only evidence they have on Luca is dating back six years ago...

Luca's team made sure that what they had was concrete evidence before Swain re questioned Luca, the concrete evidence they had found was that the old investigator was indeed corrupt. Lieutenant Swain and Mr Lavine's team spoke not only over the phone but in person as well, even with Swain wanting the conviction she knows that by rights Luca's team could make a formal complaint and they didn't hang around... Lieutenant Swain understood their frustration but when an article was published about this the media followed with great interest, Luca's solicitor had also found no DNA from Luca on any of the victims... The solicitor was not only claiming a wrongful arrest but also claiming the police would owe Luca some compensation,

At the appeal hearing Luca's team put forward the evidence they had found, the prosecutor put his side across before her ladyship made her decision... Three and a half hours later court resumed her ladyship spoke and she was disgruntled with how the case had been handled, she squashed the jury's original decision and then went onto say "I will be ordering this for a new trial and Mr Lavine is to remain in custody until then...."

"Luca this is good for us... Because now with a new trial set, we head into court knowing you are innocent in all of this..."

Lieutenant Swain was facing more pressure now for a new conviction, just as we had moved on Smithy and myself got news a new trial was happening, and they wanted us to give evidence again my solicitor explained on why this was happening the question was could I face that again? Swain went back to the very start with the case to see what she had missed then she finds something, Swain was about to put the final nail in the coffin with what she had found due to some miracle... Lieutenant Swain questioned Luca again before showing what she had found only moments ago it was CCTV footage showing Luca killing the victims, Swain sat back in her chair smiling before charging Luca of them murders.. Luca's solicitor could not believe his eyes they were confident the police would not find anything; Luca was charged with 25 different accounts of murder he was then later charged with 6 different accounts of money laundering and further charged with two different accounts of sexual assault, while under questioning Luca was then charged with sex trafficking...

Luca's solicitor wanted to look over the CCTV footage as this wasn't clear and they were unsure whether it was Luca, they even questioned the 25 different accounts of murders... When Swain's boss asked if she had covered her back, she answered with "Yes sir," not realising Luca's solicitor had been listening...

Swain had some questions from Luca's solicitor about what they had heard, and the sad news keep coming, the mental health report had also come back... Upon looking at the CCTV footage the footage was not that clear but clear enough to know it was not Luca, so the murder charges were later dropped along with the mental health report saying Mr Lavine was unfit to be questioned and was to be released... And to make Lieutenant Swain's job more difficult the solicitor asked to see the bank accounts, Lieutenant Swain knew that Lavine's solicitor was not going to allow them to walk into the court and make up lies again...

The solicitor was unhappy with how the police was acting, that is when they asked for an independent officer to take this case on... In the end Luca's case was dropped and he walked away a free man, Luca thanked the solicitor before opening his car door and driving away into the sunset...

After the FUCK UP the police made with Luca's case the police made some drastic changes... "Smithy I want to thank you for taking me in when no one else would... This city doesn't have anything here anymore for me, so I am moving back to London tonight..." While packing, my phone rang I sent the call to voicemail, Smithy asked "are you sure about this?" I answered back "no I am not sure about anything anymore, Smithy, I want you to know that whatever happens you have me as a friend for sure..."

Smithy packed the last boxes into Paul's car before turning to me and giving me an affectionate hug, "Paul you take good care of her you understand me?" As we were about to pull out the street, I see Smithy crying until Paul takes my hand that turns my attention to him... In the departure lounge I remembered about the call that I never answered when playing the voicemail, the voice on the other end was Luca's voice asking me to forgive him and take him back...

New Orleans had become my new home for now... I came here with a new Identity and no one knowing anything about me or my history, to them back in Seattle I was known as Luca Lavine here they will know me as Luca Hamilton... Since being here Edison had come to work for me and Naomi had also joined us, even though sometimes I do think about Emily and what she might be like now... I know at some point my troubles will follow me but for now I am a new person, some nights I wake screaming remembering Luca, this has been happening since coming back to London... But now I am back home I had the urge to want to take my role back within the family, when asking the family, they turned me away they said that due to me marrying someone that was involved in scandal and drugs made the family look bad...

"Hey, Boss this just came in it turns out Emily is back in London and is that Paul with her?" Seeing that Paul and Emily are now playing happy families makes me want to kill them, I needed Edison to report everything they were doing so I sent him over to London to watch them...

The obsession on wanting Emily back in my life was stronger than ever before.... I needed something strong to take this obsession away, when no one was around I pulled out the mac-book to see what Emily had been doing since back in London... That is when something showed up it was Paul holding something, the picture I zoomed in on and that gave me the answer I needed to know... It was like I had thought Emily had welcomed our son and was letting someone else play daddy to him.

Chapter 12

Seeing this made me frustrated and was not helping the obsession, that is when I drew a line of coke making me unaware of anything that was happening... The reason the case had been dropped is due to the media and the story's that was coming out with, some of them was not even linked to the case the police soon came into the light when someone decided to re look at everything... The media made a meal out this and that is when I received a pay out from them compensateding the arrest, Edison waited for Swain to leave her house before kidnapping her... Edison pulls into the warehouse with Swain eyes covered over and her hands tied behind her back, I made Swain suffer some pain before uncovering her eyes... "Mr Lavigne I would highly recommended whatever you are planning don't do it," of course Swain told me that I would end up going down for this but the red miss had taken over...

Watching Swain plead with me was highly amusing to watch, Edison covered her eyes back over before carrying out the indecent assault... I then pulled the gun out holding it to Swain's head before blowing her brains out I watched her take her last breath before she dies, we make sure that when someone comes across her all that would remain is her skeleton...

I then turn the attention to Marsdon he was next... Somehow, we made it into the palace it was not long before we came across Marsdon, Marsdon was like how you have gotten in my home before anymore was said Marsdon fell to the floor covered in his own blood...

Edison pulled Marsdon dead caucus out of the palace and into the back of the car, we went 40 miles away from Swain skeleton... The following day the news headlines was about Swain and Marsdon, missing everyone was more concerned for the king then they were about Swain... Edison and myself helped the police with their investigation, that is when I smiled and remembered Marsdon had been crushed along with the old car... It was thanks to the people that owned the place that Marsdon body was found, with people still looking for Swain I headed to see Emily...

When Emily came face to face with me, she asked "why are have you shown up now?" For you I replied she takes a long sigh before asking, "I guess you want to talk now you are a free man?" Emily then makes eye contact with me that is when I ask, "is now a good time to talk?"

"Luca understand that we are only talking because I want answers from you." Emily explained that she has not gotten over what she did to Caroline, "oh Emily how did we end up at this point? You made me the better man then what I have become, and I want you to understand that I am sorry..."

"They are words that you have used one to many times before Luca..."

Edison then interrupts us Emily stands up with fear in her eyes, "Edison can't this wait?" In that second Emily raps her arms around my waist... "Hey sweet cheeks he's gone," we rub our noses together before our lips are locked together in a passionate kiss... Emily then goes to pull down my jeans before I stop her and ask, "what are you doing?"

"Oh, I'm sorry I got carried away int that second..."

"All you must do is ask Emily and this would be yours again," Emily then asked me to leave but before I go, I answer back with "you never complained before..." What about Paul, she asked me "who gives a shit what he might think Emily we are still married," that maybe so but I am with Paul now she replies as I go to leave Emily pulls me back to her before kissing me again... I needed the time to think as we kissed more than once it was like someone had pulled the plug, and I was falling from the sky with no one to even stop me from falling at the speed that I was falling at...

A few days later the kiss that we shared had me thinking, could it work with Luca after all this time "Emily since I came back you have not been the same... Is something going on that you have not told me about has Luca shown up or has he been calling you?" Nothing happened I replied, Paul's eyes narrowed before he said, "you and him had a moment, didn't you?" We ended up kissing I replied, "YOU ARE FUCKING BITCH Emily what we have is something good and you want to go back to him?"

"He turned up wanting to talk and it ended up with us kissing more than once Paul, I told him I am with you now don't turn this into something...."

Chapter 13

Seeing Paul almost broken due to me kissing Luca more than once, made me relies on kissing Luca came as a mistake and he was my pass and not the future.... When Luca called asking to see me again my head was saying one thing, and my heart was saying another... "Luca what is happening with Emily and you? Is she coming back to you or what because she could end up talking, and we need her to keep shut about what you really do wouldn't you agree with me?" Emily knows she cannot do talk to anyone I replied she not even answering my phone calls I went on I called her again but nothing, I headed to the house but on arriving I see Paul's SUV in the driveway I took my chance knowing this could end badly... Paul answers the door I get a frosty response he looks and then calls Emily, "what are you doing turning up why Paul is here?" Paul watches from the kitchen making sure nothing goes on with us...

"Luca I might not like you, but Emily needs stability and so does Michael..."

I put my hand out for Paul to shake but he walks away, "Emily can we talk about me seeing Michael? I am not asking for much from you..." Just give a me a second, she replies she goes and gets Michael and for a moment I stand looking at the boy that is my son... Emily hands Michael to me and she explains that I am his daddy, "he's like you in every way Luca..." Really, I replied before Paul says "it's time you was on your way come back another time and we will talk more..."

"Emily, I want you to know that with Luca showing up here we can't be together... I understand that you and he have history but after all he put you through, how can you even consider going there again with him?" Anyone that I have ever loved has done this to me I replied... "Do you want me to move out the house?" Yes, but Michael stays here with me I answer back with, "SORRY WHAT Michael is my son me and Luca created him so no he comes with me..." Do you remember the last time we were in London together Emily we got down and dirty together and it wasn't long after you fell pregnant, I replied! "How could I forget having you put that length in me made me sick Luca has more of a length then you," I go to call Luca he answers almost right away and ask, "Emily what's wrong?"

"Paul is kicking me out the house but he wanting to keep Michael," hold on I'm coming he replied Emily came running out the door and into my arms... Edison got Michael as we pulled up at home Emily says, "I was wrong for leaving you..."

"Hey, it's fine let's go in doors we can talk more there..."

That evening Emily and I spoke for hours making new house rules and coming up with an agreement, that everyone was able to agree on...

The following morning over breakfast Luca sat me down and explained, on what he and Edison had done to Marsdon that is when I asked about Swain? For some reason I was not even mad over Marsdon, I was more interested in whether they had killed Swain... By now Swain case had gone cold Marsdon's case on the other hand police was still investigating, but that morning got even more interesting when the police made an arrest and was questioning someone on suspicion of murder for killing Marsdon and Swain... It turned out the police had two 18-year-old men in questioning, nothing came from the police on whether the two men had been let go or charged...

People was now growing increasingly concerned about Swain and why no one had seen her, with the police now letting the two 18-year-old men walk free... The police did come out and explained that they were going to do a TV appeal for any information on the case, "our daughter has been missing for six weeks and if anyone has any information on where she might be phoning the number on screen..."

"Edison tonight we move her the police are now searching that area," what are you going to tell Emily he asked "don't worry about that now let me take care of Emily..." Edison came unstuck when he went to move Swain as the police had everything cornered off, Edison had spotted the police had gotten something with forensic about two yards away from the shallow grave... That night the police arrested Edison for murdering Marsdon and on suspicion of murdering Swain, they couldn't get him on Swain, but they had him for Marsdon... The police then released a statement saying they had formerly charged someone on killing the king, Edison know not to drop my name into any of this that was going on...

The police ended up founding nothing in the area that they were searching, it was only when they were packing away that one drug dog came across something... It happened to be Swain card then the dog went digging but ended up founding nothing, Edison pleaded not guilty to murdering Marsdon the coroner's report said that Marsdon was dead before the gun was shot... "Before you send me down you need to know that I was not acting alone that night I was with Luca Hamilton aca Lavigne," that is when the police went into questioning me about Marsdon, but I was soon let go...

Emily couldn't help but think was history about to repeat itself when I had told her it want, all we now could do is wait and see what happened....

The new investigating officers that were now dealing with the Marsdon and Swain case, went looking into why the case with me was dropped... They soon found that the evidence they looked at had no forensics evidence to support the case that they had against me at the time, they keep looking and they looked at the CCTV footage with better quality, but they weren't going to rest in till they worked it out...

They came and asked questions that had me worrying about them reopening my case...

"We can't bring him back in he has been investigated more than once, but depending on what the fraud squad found we might be able to on that keep me updated on this night..." Boss this case with Lavigne is they more to this than what we might think I asked, "let's talk to Edison he might know something but go carefully, we don't want to lose our jobs or end up dead do we now?" The police now could open a new case on me over fraud and sex trafficking, the police spoke to the victims, and they found that all the victims had been a housekeeper or once worked with me... The police were than informed not to take any action with this case, as it would be too risky to follow up on and that I would do lawsuit for the second time...

They weren't impressed that they had a convincing case to take to court, and the CPS had said no to carrying out the case till the end...

Chapter 14

The officers had been told no and they were sure if it went to court, they would get a conviction I on the other hand was somewhat happy the police didn't carry out the case... Edison had been given the maximum sentence for murdering Marsdon, Emily had her own thoughts on them giving the maximum sentence but deep down she wanted more than anyone else for Edison to walk free... That is when my old, trusted assistant shows up Paul had come to pick Michael up for the night, Emily rubs her nose against mine before moving in for a kiss her hands trail down my chest before she then opens my zipper... I stop her for a moment and asked, "are you 100% sure you want to do this?"

She whispers quietly into my ear "yes," making me chuckle before pulling down my nicely ironed suit trousers I carry her into the bedroom with only her panties on... I then gently suck on her nipple before laying her down on the bed the bedroom has had a little update since the last time, we were together I then pull down my blue boxer shorts revealing my length to her...

I make my way up the bed before putting my length insider her; after making out Emily turns to me and speaks "I have missed this with us..."

Sure, you have I say quietly knowing her head was laying on my naked chest, I tend to keep my chest hair shaven as some women don't like it... "Hey I want to ask you something how would you feel about me having my role back with in my family?" His eyes narrowed at the question his brow furrowed before, letting out an exasperating breath "kill this moment why don't you Emily... We have just fucked, and you want to take your role back in your family FUCK THAT sleep on your own tonight..." I was only asking a question Luca I replied "NO you asked that to piss me off and you have done that, remember Emily why you wanted out the family and remember this you are nothing without me..."

He leaves me crying as he walks out the door, I head into the bathroom and lock the door sometime after Luca says, "Emily are you okay?" His voice was softer than before I open to see him holding what looks to be a mug of tea for me, "SORRY Emily I should have not gone off at you like that..."

"You need to keep that temper in check, remember I am your wife not someone that you picked up from the street even though you did pick me up of the street..." His eyes darken a little but not to the point of him losing that temper again he pulls me into his chest before laying a kiss on my lips, "Emily, I got an appointment with a therapist next week to help me understand my anger more..."

"Well, that is something and do you want me to come with you?"

He chuckles before answering with "I'll be fine on my own..."

Luca's facial expression said what I needed to know; this was a man that was abandoned through no fault of his own and had been passed around from an early age... Luca made his own way in this world unlike me that had been given everything that I wanted, "Boss I know you told us not to keep looking at the case but something has made us want to question Mr Lavigne about this..." I grunt at this before telling them to bring him in for questioning, we made sure that Luca know he was not under any caution and could go at any time...

Mr Habib Luca's representative wasted no time on letting us know, his client has spent more time here than was necessary and asked that we made this quick...

Habib had been doing this for nearly 45 years or more he was well equipped to how the law was, Habib was approaching retirement... Our boss looked and under his breath said told you so, before walking away and moving on to the next case...

Chapter 15

"Luca tell me why you are here today?" The therapist asked but when thinking about it my mind went foggy, Emily explained that I had anger problems and a little drug problem... Miss Windsor made notes on what we spoke about that is when she asked Emily to step out the room, "I was abandoned no one would even look at me my real mother and father gave me up... Caroline and Edison lied but when they took me on Edison had been kicked out the family home due to Caroline, "thanks for opening up that couldn't have been easy for you?" As I stand to walk out the room and all too familiar feeling takes on over in that second, I turn to the therapist and speak "you have no idea on what I am capable of...." The therapist moves uncomfortably with the sudden fret that was made from Luca; the therapist eyes watch him carefully before Luca leaves the room... "why threaten someone like that?"

Late that night why sleeping Luca begun calling out in his sleep, he was calling for Caroline and Smithy I wake when he begins hitting out... In this moment Luca is now heavily sweating I know then that the dream had become worser then what it was some time ago, the dream had taken him back to the night I killed Caroline when he wakes, he sees me looking concerned more than normal "do you want to talk about this Emily?" My eyes roll when he asked do I want to talk about it, before answering with "yeah sure..."

At around 11.30pm that evening two police officers showed up at the house, they wanted me to accompany them to the station... The officers explained that some added information had become known about the Caroline case the added information was that the gun had been fined, the forensics was not long coming back with a DNA match of course my DNA was all over the gun... The officer spoke with his sergeant and suggested due to me being linked to royals that it was not advisable to take this case to court, the sergeant wanted to pursue with the case...

Due to the nature of the case and how complex it was the officers, made the decision to not prosecute... By now our patience with the federal government had run out, once outside I pull my cell phone out my back pocket only to have sixteen calls from an upset husband... Before I known anything Luca's car was pulling up in front of me his eyes were dark, and his expression said what I needed to know...

"Leave us alone now!" them worlds echo around the house... Luca then removes his strap from around his waist in this second, I know what was about to happen he walks on over to me... He then whispers into my ear before he placed my hand on his length, "when are you going to learn not to defy me?"

Luca then rips my top open revealing my chest before removing my bra... "That's what I like to see a woman's boobs hanging out now" I want to shout for help, but I don't instead I let him carry on why holding back the tears once he had done, he goes into the bathroom to clean up... I then run across the hallway to find some new bras once dressed I call 911 to get some help, the police take me down to the station because they wanted to know more on what has happened... "I thought he had change I guess I was wrong, what will happen now I asked?" Due to the complex of us being married it came down to my word against his, this time we were not going back to that house we were heading back to London... News had gotten out due to unpaid tax all that Luca possessed was now owned by the bailiffs, the figgier that was being reported was a substantial amount of money his house and cars was now gone due to this...

Luca had a meeting with his legal team and his accountant, he made his feelings known and simply put the blame on his accountant... It turns out that Emily had given the accountant power of attorney, Emily had simply screwed her husband over for the last time... Emily wanted to show her husband that you hurt her and her family this was what you call pay back, Luca's house and cars went to auction he was also looking at a prison sentence for this unpaid tax... The bailiffs had gotten involved when Luca's accountant had seen suspicious activity, in Luca's accounts, the officer that was now investigating this case wanted to question Luca about this....

The investigation officer now had the paperwork they needed... Luca was looking up to five years in prison if he was convicted in the court of law the unpaid tax dated back to 1999, when the officer showed the paperwork in the interview room to Luca and his legal team his legal team said "that signature is not my clients..." All the evidence was strong against Luca, the officer denied police bail and wood keep Lavigne on remand Luca was now spitting feathers at what the officer was saying to him...

I sat in my new house in London and watched the news following this story with Luca... I made sure before handing things over to his accountant I took what was owed to me, and made sure the police couldn't trace it me pulling this out on my own husband were heart broking...

Luca's legal team asked the officer weather they had spoken to Emily, as his legal team had traced the signature back to Emily... Luca's team had also somehow managed to account for some of the money, the money raised from selling everything had not even paid half on the unpaid tax... The police spoke with people that worked with Luca and they said they was unaware of any problems, with the evidence the officer now had regarding this case he went to the cps to find out whether they would prosecute...

Because Luca known that the money was blood money, he didn't put the money that he made in his accounts so the accountant was unaware of this money... Luca managed to keep this money away from people that might happen to talk to the tax man, Luca would very often with the money filter it so when the money came back in some way or another it would be clean... Luca wanted to make sure Emily and his son had some security if anything happened to him, yes he was using the money he made from whatever he did...

Luca had seen this happen in a film that he once watched... Luca know if anyone asked about it that they would be chasing his imagination, Luca would sometimes use the money and tie it up in some investments and no one had any idea on were the money came from...

This was known as a tax scandal that happens a lot in this world... Tax scandal has been happing for decades some get away with it and some do not, it came to people's attention when Luca gave a lot of money to Naomi for his ill son that is when suspicions was raised to the tax man... It turns out that the tac man happened to be in the same area when Luca gave Naomi the money, the new apartment the family had gotten for me overlooked the river thames the apartment had marble work tops... The flooring of the apartment when you walked into it had a sand effect throughout the apartment, the windows had like a nice red velvet curtain from the ceiling to the floor... They were like a fireplace splitting the living room from the dining room, being away from Luca and his henchman gave me time to think and to put what had happened into perspective...

Knowing that now they were only me and Michael here... I set out to make things right with an old friend that friend was Paul, coming home was right for me when looking back they was no hope of surviving the mental torment of what was happening with them... Once setting the restraining order gave me the power to take back not only control but my entire life and it was needed so long ago, "Emily this unexpected... Come in how are you? And how is this little one doing?"

"You were right about him I shouldn't have gone back..." Seeing Paul's eyes light up with enjoyment that I was back

with him gave me the satisfaction that had been needed,
Paul and I spoke for hours we even watched the evening sun
set over the river thames...

Chapter 16

We sat under the evening moon before we broke apart for the night... I had to head back to Seattle to give the news that I now wanted to divorce him and never see him again, why seeing Luca the police gave me a letter asking me to give evidence in court... When looking at the letter the court date was tomorrow, I explained it to Paul, and he would look after Michael... Only this time they were no corruption with the police, this might be the last time Luca name ever comes up for a long time....

With Luca pleading guilty he would be looking at a lighter sentence... Luca owed the tax man up to $ 999.50046 million in tac's, on day number one in court the court room was standing only once court had gotten underway... The Luca we were seeing in court was not the one people know he was acting; this was not a case that would done in a few days this case was going to be weeks... Somehow Luca had managed to find someone to make a documentary on him, I would have stayed around for the case but after giving my evidence I had to get back to London to see Michael and Paul... His legal team gave it their all and they pulled a massive cat out the bag they could now account for every single Doller, that had been spent they even went to the extent on showing the court their spreadsheet...

The prosecution asked the court a question, "how's is it that Mr Lavigne's legal team can now account for all the money? When Mr Lavigne was questioned, they couldn't even account for some of the money never mined all of it?"

The question made not only the people in the gallery think but also the jury, before her ladyship asked, "why this spreadsheet was not presented as evidence before now?" Her ladyship wanted time to go over this new evidence that his legal team had shown in the court, after hours spent going over the new evidence repeatedly, she would allow it to be used in court... Luca's odds was now at 99% he would walk away a free man due to this new evidence that his legal team had come up with, it were now down to the jury on whether he would walk away or go down...

This case had divided the jury down the middle... They had to have a majority before heading back into court the jury came to a majority now it was time the verdict, the jury had been out for around 64 hours that was 9 weeks and 1 day...

The tv cameras from across the world had their eyes on this case... When the jury was sent to deliberate, we back in the UK waited for news, as days passed the unknowing was becoming unsettling for everyone... The jury were convinced that Luca had no part in this, but between them they were convinced it was Luca's accountant that was to blame...

Every day when looking over the evidence it was clear that it was indeed Luca's accountant... The jury could not go to her ladyship and say that they believed it was the accountant, all the evidence that had been given to the jury had Luca's accountant name on it the only evidence that had Luca's name on it were the spreadsheet...

That gave the jury the majority they needed; the evidence did calls disagreements at times they were the odd three that believed no matter what the evidence was saying to them, believed that Luca was guilty they would not agree with the other members of the jury... To start with others did think the same thing, but when the spreadsheet was given to them that is when they understand something clearly at last... At points, the jury had to cool them self's down with each other, the court asked on if they had come to a majority the answer was a "yes" that is when they do you find Luca Lavigne "guilty or not guilty?" The tension could be cut with a knife in the court when the answer came back as "guilty" everyone was shocked, in the gallery Luca's accountant smiled with joy knowing what he had done...

They sentence Luca to 18 months at her majesty pleasure...

The accountant after the sentencing ran to the bathroom to be sick... His mutters under his breath "that was close thank God, they find him guilty," Unknown to the accountant Luca's legal team happened to be in the next cubicle and had heard what the accountant had said... Due to them hearing that and had recorded them saying that they went and launched an appeal, the hunt was now to locate this accountant that been dealing with Luca's money they was stacks of paperwork that was used in court... I went over the paperwork must have been sixteen or more time that I cannot remember, one little thing did stand out to me and that was the accountant had used other names that was not his...

I gave the police a call and told them about this... This person didn't even exist apart from on paper, the police run the accountant's name through their databases... The real name of the accountant happened to be someone called D'Amore but that was not the name on the paperwork, the named used is someone made up we put the word about that we wanted to speak to this D'Amore...

Once people know we wanted to speak with this D'Amore we got several people, reporting that they had fallen into the same situation as what Luca was now in... Those people were willing to make statements and even testify in court that this D'Amore is nothing but a con artist, those people went and made statements to the police and the officer dealing with the case put out a warrant for his arrest... Luca couldn't understand how we had managed to work out that it was D'Amore and not him, the las time anyone had seen this D'Amore was not long after Luca had been sent down...

We had people checking his bank account and no money had been deposited for a while now... The las transaction was the day that Luca were due in court, D'Amore had planned this he must have known that we were onto him as his boss had not seen him since that day...

At around 9pm on a Saturday evening the police picked D'Amore's wife up.... She answered the questions and that is when she told us that she had made a missing person report, the officer was not aware of this report being made he asked his boss on weather he was aware of it? The officers looked at each other before calling time on asking her questions... Since coming home to London I had forgotten about the name Lavigne, "Emily... Someone is here to see you about this D'Amore?" Send them in thanks Paul I replied, "Miss Lavigne thanks for seeing us you don't happen to have any bank statements, would you?" Sorry, what is this about I replied... Paul comes walking in the room to see me upset, Paul ordered the officers to stop the questions...

Paul wipes away the tears with his rough hands making me almost quiver at the knees... Paul's skin seems lighter than what I remember, but when looking into them eyes you see a hall different world to the one, we are now living in...

"Paul did you suffer when your wife passed away ten years ago?" His eyes filled with tears and the emotion came flooding out... "Rose died due to childbirth, and I didn't only loss her that night but I also loss Rose Junior they said they might have been a chance if Rose had not have been ill..." He goes on to say, "after Rose died my world fell apart but Luca saved me that night," we share a kiss before Michael pulls us apart... Rose came to the us to find a man when she got here her English was not good, Rose was Puerto Rican her skin was so soft to the touch somewhat like Emily's....

Rose came to the Brooklyn when she was sixteen years old, she had nothing when she came here, we meet a year later some say Rose married me for the convenience of her staying in the us.... The legal team to Luca had now come up with another plan to find this D'Amore, Luca had become frustrated that nothing had been done and he know that deep down he was actually innocent in this...

By now Luca was wanting answers on why they had not found this D'Amore...

Chapter 17

D'Amore had been spotted walking in the city via some people... Time they had informed the police he had gone the police did another credit card check, only to find money has gone into his account and had also been taken out the account the same day... Being unable to have the control that I am so use to having is somewhat demoralising and knowing that at this point the control is with someone else, the thing you never get use to is when the lights go out and you are alone with them thought... And sometimes you want to end it all but a man that looks hard on the outside is utterly terrified on the inside and at some point, the control is given back to you...

You come to realize on the inside you are not the top dog anymore, and to come into places and take what they own you are asking for trouble... Since being locked up in here you must watch your back, I have had the FUCK kicked out of me why being locked up...

When being placed in the holding cell unaware of anything that is happening outside... Is very unsettling because in here that control has been taken away from you, it turns out that this D'Amore had now been taken in for questioning about his money activities... He was to be transferred back to London with in 24 hours as he was court by the Portuguese police, on arriving back in England he was meet with Sky news and other news people covering the story...

D'Amore was taken into custody and asked on whether he could make a call to someone... D'Amore called his solicitor they turned up within one hour of the call being made to them, "Mr Amore as your solicitor I want you to refrain from answering any questions do you understand?" Yes, he replied to the solicitor the solicitor then turned to the officer and requested to see the paperwork... D'Amore sat back and watched his solicitor make a dog's dinner on what the police was asking, "I would like us to continue this once Mr Amore has had some sleep don't you agree officers?"

"They can only keep you for 48 hours after that they have to let you go...." It was a long 48 hours down at the police station for D'Amore and his solicitor, D'Amore was then formally charged with fraud... The solicitor was under the impression that D'Amore was a victim of cohesive control, "Emily have been told the police have D'Amore?"

"What does that mean for Luca?" It means that at some point he will walk away Paul replied for a second, I was hoping for a different answer to what Paul gave me... Knowing that creep would be walking free would have me questioning everything that I did or wanted to do, D'Amore pleaded not guilty to fraud his solicitor had convinced the court that D'Amore was indeed a victim of cohesive control...

The court now wanted concrete evidence that this was true...

This was going to be difficult for D'Amore's solicitor, but the solicitor had done something like this before with another case... The solicitor looked back on an old case to see what he did in that case, once Luca know that D'Amore was now locked up... Luca hope to see the scum bag that costed him everything, and once he had been told he was heading to the same cell block as him his eyes filled with anger... Luca had arranged to have this D'Amore sexual assaulted, the officers assured D'Amore nothing would happen to him that afternoon in the courtyard Luca came face to face with D'Amore...

Luca lowered D'Amore into a false sense of security, before the assault happened D'Amore had put up a fight but lose Luca came from the darkness and chuckled... Before laying a beat down to D'Amore, "you messed with the fucking wrong person ASS HOLL!"

"Next time you cross me I will kill you got it?"

D'Amore informed his solicitor about the assault and the solicitor took this to the police... "Mr D'Amore your solicitor says you was assaulted, is that right?"

"Yes, and he said next time he would kill me..."

"Who said this to you?"

"Lavigne!"

"Thank you, Mr D'Amore, and this should not have happened..." Photos was taken from the assault and a statement was also given, the police questioned Luca over the assault the officers soon realised the motive behind the assault and then charged Luca with the assault... The second charges were for the same thing but with people unknown, "EM is something wrong the guard said it was urgent?"

"Sit down and I will explain everything to you? The Hamilton family wanted me to come and tell you, that due to who you are and how you go about your business... They are removing you from the line of succession," go back to them and tell them to FUCK THEM SELFS he replied... "Oh EM before you I love you?" Your sick I say back before walking away, "How did he take the news Emily?"

"Same old Same old Luca everything must be about him, take me home Paul..." Luca had been given additional time add on to his 18 months sentence, when D'Amore's case went to trial and given all that he had done to people and what had happened he would only be doing 7.5 of a 15 year sentence...

The head of the Hamilton family came to speak with me... They asked me on whether I would consider becoming the new queen? The Hamilton family were willing to overlook what had happened, they also stated that Micheal was to be named as a prince from now on... After some consideration I accepted the offer with the condition that Paul would be known as a king? "Emily what about you wanting to be independent?" Paul asked he had a good point, but the family need me right now I replied, this power came with great responsibilities, and I was determined to make our family meaningful again...

Chapter 18

Six weeks into being the queen and I was facing chaos with America wanting, to invade on another country now I understand why mother sometimes didn't like being queen... When think back to when mother was queen and the tales, she would tell us were fascinating... The Hamilton family wanted to bring prestige back not only to the monarchy but also to the family name, and when you look at the kings that came before us and the same for the queens you would have hope they would not be any corruption, but there are... Mother when she was queen wanted to end this corruption and give woman there voice that they wanted, I only took being queen because the Hamilton family didn't have anyone that was old enough...

A local newspaper had somehow found out that I was once married to a killer, this newspaper seen that they were a story to be made from me being married to a killer... The newspaper made a headline saying, "future queen in danger," they weren't wrong about that but as queen now I was unable to comment on the headline... A spoke person for the family didn't deny it or confirm it, the Hamilton's wanted the spoke person to shut this newspaper down as it was nothing to do with them...

"EM do you have a second?"

"Yeah, sure what's up?"

"With everything that has happened, I wanted to know on whether you were free tonight?"

"Oh, you want some attention sure 8pm okay for you?"

Paul walks away smiling trying to hide the boner that he has right now, that night when we were alone in our chamber Paul comes walking on over undoing his night robe... I couldn't think when a man had last touch me, so I was going to enjoy this moment... Paul then removes the black nightwear that covered me up, he lays my naked body on the Lennon bedding, before crawling between my legs and placing his length inside of me making me scream out... We continued into the night and fell asleep as the sun came up, "Hmm are you now satisfied Paul?"

"You were like a dog on heat he answers back with," Emily through a little smile in Paul's direction agreeing with him before they were interrupted from a house made... Paul slowly removes himself from the bedding before pulling me closer to him hoping the house made would not see his crown jewels, as the house made left the chamber we was then alone for a moment... In till the made came back into the room with a letter, the letter was from Luca asking whether we can talk about Micheal?

I read the letter time and time again trying to understand what he was asking?

Suddenly I find myself going through the prison security knowing that he might not show up... I waited for nearly 15 minutes before someone said that he was not coming, he would have known that I would come so for him not turning up he was playing games with me... "Hello Em how are?" The husky voice means he has decided to come and talk with me, but the conversation didn't last long as time was called...

Chapter 19

Only if he had shown up sooner, we might have been able to talk more about how he could see Micheal once he was out that place... His expression said what I needed to know, and the expression was mind games he wasn't able to pull them puppet strings to make me dance anymore... And deep down he knows that and that frustrated Luca knowing he was unable to pull them strings, his eyes filled with anger knowing that deep down he was not able to control this situation...

I was wanting to keep this situation away from the courts but with us unable to agree... The courts would now decide on when Luca would be able to see Micheal, all that was needed was Luca to agree but he made this decision to take it to the family courts.... Micheal was the innocent party in this case and for whatever reason Luca was making this about him like he always does

Christmas Day 2040

This Christmas is going to haunt us for years to come...

To be continue in Love Child

Recognition to the people that help with this book

- **Peter John McPhail – Father**
- **Karen McPhail – Mother**
- **Support Workers (FitzRoy**
- **Suzanne Neil (Social Worker**
- **Cloe Parke – Friend**

Thank you to everyone that contributed and supported me on drafting this book... As it wouldn't have been possible without your support And any money made from this book will be going to the dog's trust